Lighthouse Christmas

story by Toni Buzzeo
pictures by Nancy Carpenter

Dial Books for Young Readers
an imprint of Penguin Group (USA) Inc.

To Ken, who watches over the mariners and shares Christmas magic with me—*T.B.*
For Mom and Dad—*N.C.*

DIAL BOOKS FOR YOUNG READERS
A division of Penguin Young Readers Group
Published by The Penguin Group
Penguin Group (USA) Inc., 375 Hudson Street, New York, NY 10014, U.S.A.

Penguin Group (Canada), 90 Eglinton Avenue East, Suite 700, Toronto, Ontario, Canada M4P 2Y3 (a division of Pearson Penguin Canada Inc.)
Penguin Books Ltd, 80 Strand, London WC2R 0RL, England
Penguin Ireland, 25 St. Stephen's Green, Dublin 2, Ireland (a division of Penguin Books Ltd)
Penguin Group (Australia), 250 Camberwell Road, Camberwell, Victoria 3124, Australia (a division of Pearson Australia Group Pty Ltd)
Penguin Books India Pvt Ltd, 11 Community Centre, Panchsheel Park, New Delhi - 110 017, India
Penguin Group (NZ), 67 Apollo Drive, Rosedale, Auckland 0632, New Zealand (a division of Pearson New Zealand Ltd)
Penguin Books (South Africa) (Pty) Ltd, 24 Sturdee Avenue, Rosebank, Johannesburg 2196, South Africa
Penguin Books Ltd, Registered Offices: 80 Strand, London WC2R 0RL, England

Text copyright © 2011 by Toni Buzzeo
Pictures copyright © 2011 by Nancy Carpenter

Designed by Nancy R. Leo-Kelly
Text set in ITC Stone Informal
10 9 8 7 6 5 4 3 2 1

Library of Congress Cataloging-in-Publication Data
Buzzeo, Toni.
Lighthouse Christmas / Toni Buzzeo ; illustrated by Nancy Carpenter.
p. cm.
Summary: Christmas is two days away, but Frances and her little brother Peter, who recently moved with their father to a lighthouse on an isolated island,
fear that they will have no treats, no music, and no visit from Santa. Includes facts about the Flying Santa Service.
ISBN 978-0-8037-3053-3 (hardcover)
[1. Christmas—Fiction. 2. Lighthouses—Fiction. 3. Brothers and sisters—Fiction.] I. Carpenter, Nancy, ill. II. Title.
PZ7.B9832Lhm 2011 [E]—dc22 2011001160

The art was prepared using a combination of pen on paper and digital media.

Morning light drifted down the curving lighthouse stairs. Peter appeared on the floor below Frances, hugging the one-eared cat. He stood smack in the pile of dirt Frances had just swept down from the top of Ledge Light tower.

"How many days 'til Christmas?" he asked.

Frances waved the broom to scoot him aside. "One less than yesterday."

"Two?"

Frances nodded.

"Will Christmas come to this island too?" Peter asked.

"I s'pose it will," said Frances.

"Good. I want Christmas," Peter said.

We both want Christmas, Frances thought. So why did people have to live in lonely places like Ledge Light?

Frances hung the broom behind the kitchen door. She could hear Papa chopping firewood outside.

"Christmas, Frances! Cookies and singing and presents," Peter piped from the rocker where he sat stroking the cat. "And Santa."

"Yes," Frances said. But she wasn't sure that Santa even knew where Ledge Light was, here in the middle of the ocean. When Mama died in spring, Papa had taken the transfer from the mainland lighthouse. Had Santa noticed?

Later, Frances found Peter in the parlor with crayons and paper scraps all around.

"I'm planning Christmas," he said, "and you can help."

Frances picked up one of the scraps. "What's *this* plan?"

"Cookie shapes," Peter said.

Frances's mouth watered at the memory of butter cookies, sweet with sugar. Then she remembered the empty larder. "Maybe not cookies this year."

She picked up another scrap.

"*Ho ho ho, the piano,*" Peter sang.

Her ears rang with the memory of Aunt Martha's beautiful playing.

"Presents for everyone," Peter said. "Even the one-eared cat."

Frances had to smile. "That old cat doesn't even know it's Christmas."

"But we do." Peter grabbed her hand. "We can *start* making Christmas and Santa can finish up."

The sound of Papa's chopping stopped outside. "Best hurry that cat outdoors, Peter," Frances warned. Too late. Snow followed Papa into the kitchen.

"Papa!" Peter rushed to him.

Papa reached out an arm, then spotted the cat. "That cat doesn't belong inside."

"But Papa," Peter chirped, "he's the Ledge Light cat—and we're the Ledge Light family now."

Without another word, Papa opened the door and shooed the cat outside.

Frances set three bowls of oatmeal on the table.

Peter tasted a spoonful. "It's not sweet today."

"No, not today." The sugar was gone, like most everything else, Frances thought. Sooner or later the weather would let up and the supply boat would arrive. But probably too late for Christmas.

Papa cleared his throat. "Aunt Martha radioed offering to send a dory out to fetch you children for Christmas."

Peter bounced in his seat. "Cookies and singing and presents and Santa for sure."

Frances gave him a tiny kick under the table. "What about you, Papa?"

Papa shook his head. "Storms threatening boats at sea don't consider holidays."

Frances felt like a boat moored to a dock.

"But can *we* go have Christmas, Frances?" Peter asked.

"You think on that a while, Frances, and let me know," Papa said.

Creak, crack. Creak, crack. The rockers squeaked out a waiting rhythm on the parlor floor as the sky darkened with storm clouds. No supply boat again today. Already, the larder echoed like a yawning beast with only a canister of oatmeal and a fifty-pound sack of beans in its stomach. *Beans for Christmas dinner?*

Frances whirled around to Peter. "Okay, we'll go!"

Peter flew across the floor and threw his arms around Frances's waist.

"Go tell Papa," Frances said, heading for her room.

Ten minutes later, Peter appeared in the doorway. "What are you doing?"

"Making a present to leave for Papa," she whispered.

"Santa brings presents for everyone everywhere—even lighthouse cats," said Peter.

The cat and Papa—alone at Christmas with the boats on the sea. She tried not to think about that as she trimmed sheets of paper evenly and bound them together with ribbon. She labeled the cardboard cover LIGHTHOUSE KEEPER'S JOURNAL.

Just then, an enormous gust of wind drove snow against the rattling window.

Oh no! Frances thought. How would they get to the mainland?

She rushed up the tower stairs and pushed into the lamp room where Papa was hurrying into his slicker. "Frances," he hollered above the howl of the wind. "Look there, just past the ledge. Do you see it?"

Frances peered through the telescope and spotted an upturned fishing boat.

Papa shoved his sou'wester on his head. "I'll try to reach him in my dory."

"No, Papa!" Frances cried.

"Frances, I must. And you must keep the light burning."

Her heart thudded. She'd never lit the wick herself.

Too soon after he'd left, a blast of wind blew out the light. Her hands shook. A gust blew out her match.

Once.

Twice.

A third time she lit the match and held it to the wick. The flame wavered. She held her breath.

When she let it out, the flame was burning. Frances peered down to the water below where Papa was dragging something over the gunnels of his dory.

It seemed like hours later when she finally saw Papa below, dragging a dripping man toward the kitchen door.

The nor'easter raged all night long. Frances hovered over the mariner. She rubbed his hands and feet, trying to chase off the bone chill of the sea.

In the morning, Peter slid into the kitchen in his pajamas. He eyed the stranger. "Are you here to take us to the mainland?"

"No sir," he said. "I'm Mr. Dunlap, the fella your papa dragged out of the sea last night—thanks to your sister keeping the light burning."

Peter turned his wide eyes on Frances. "You did?"

"We're the lighthouse family," Frances said, pouring tea for Mr. Dunlap. "I had to."

"But we're going ashore today, right, Frances?"

Frances glanced away. "Maybe not, Peter," she whispered.

Peter's smile crumpled, and he ran from the room.

Frances and the cat followed. Peter lay curled in a tight ball on the bed. He reached out to pet the cat but refused to look at Frances.

"I'm sorry," she said. "But remember what you told Papa the other day?"

He lay still. "What?"

"We're the lighthouse family now—the Ledge Light family." Frances combed her fingers through Peter's hair. "If it weren't for me, Mr. Dunlap would be dead at the bottom of the sea, Peter. Papa and I saved him. That's what lighthouse keepers do."

Peter rolled over. "But can lighthouse keepers have Christmas too?"

"Oh, I think they can!"

In the kitchen, Mr. Dunlap was asleep by the stove.

Frances tapped Peter's shoulder and whispered, "I'm putting you in charge of a gift for Mr. Dunlap. Santa might not be able to find him."

"I'll do it," Peter agreed, heading for his room.

"He's part of the Ledge Light family today," Frances called after him.

"Just like the one-eared cat," Peter answered.

By afternoon, the storm slid up the coast. Peter and Frances went out to find a green pine bough. They dragged it inside to the parlor and laid their gifts beneath.

"No cookies," Peter said.

"No piano music," Frances added.

"But we have a little Christmas anyway," said Peter.

Frances squeezed his hand. "Yes, we do."

"Let's get Papa and Mr. Dunlap," said Peter.

"Better give the cat his gift first, then put him out," Frances said.

Peter and Frances led Papa and Mr.
Dunlap into the parlor. Together they sang
"Jingle Bells" as best they could without
Aunt Martha's piano music.

At the end of the song, Frances heard a
roaring noise outside. "Listen!" she said.

They rushed out.

A small plane circled low above the lighthouse.

It circled a second time.

Then the plane dipped and banked to one side and swooped past. A package fell out of the tail and landed at the water's edge.

Inside was a thick layer of marsh hay wrapped around a heavy burlap sack.

Peter hopped from one foot to another as Papa carried the sack into the house. "Santa sent a plane!"

"Yes," said Frances, her eyes wide, "he did."

Frances pulled treasure after treasure from the bag—tins of coffee, tea, cocoa, and sugar, crayons, jacks, yo-yos, books, and a Bible.

Peter clapped. "Now there's *more* Christmas—from Santa."

Papa shook his head in wonderment.

Frances reached into the bag one last time and removed a note:

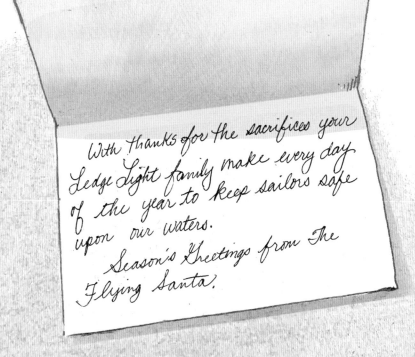

With thanks for the sacrifices your Ledge Light family make every day of the year to keep sailors safe upon our waters.
Season's Greetings from The Flying Santa.

"I'll second that!" boomed Mr. Dunlap.

Papa wrapped his strong arms around Frances and Peter.
"My Ledge Light family!"

From outside came a yowl and a scratch at the door.

Everyone waited for Papa.

He rubbed his chin and laughed. "That cat . . ."

". . . is part of our Ledge Light family!" Peter said as he
flung the door open and let the one-eared cat inside.

Author's Note

On Christmas Day 1929, floatplane pilot William Wincapaw launched the Flying Santa Service
to honor the many lighthouse keepers and their families he'd come to know on the isolated islands in
Maine's Penobscot Bay. He delivered packages filled with holiday gifts of small necessities and luxuries
by dropping them from his plane to the lights in the Rockland area. Over the years, the flights expanded
into other states, first in New England and then across the continent. As the tradition grew, expenses
were underwritten by businesses, and other Flying Santas followed Bill, including famed maritime
historian and author Edward Rowe Snow. With the exception of the war years, 1941–1944, the Flying
Santa service has been continually active from 1929 until the present, now visiting Coast Guard families
as the tradition continues.

To learn more about the Flying Santa Service, visit www.flyingsanta.com.

NOV 2011